Ruffles

and the red, red coat

David Melling

This is **Ruffles.**

Ruffles **loves . . .**

singing . . .

scratching . . .

eating . . .

fetching . . .

sniffing . . .

chewing . . .

digging . . .

running . . .

and sleeping.

But Ruffles **does not love** his new coat.

Not one . . .   teeny, tiny . . .   little bit.

No.   No.   No.

No.   No.   No.

Ruffles should wear his coat
when it is cold and wet.

Today, it is cold and wet . . .

and the rain is making puddles.

Ruffles **loves** puddles.

So Ruffles sniffs . . .   and pats . . .   and licks . . .

and splishes . . .   and splashes . . .   and sploshes . . .

and jumps . . .   and jumps . . .   and jumps . . .

without his coat.

Here is Ruffles' friend, Ruby!

Ruby's wearing her smart new coat!

They sniff . . .

and pat . . .

and lick . . .

and splish . . .

and splash . . .

and splosh . . .

and jump . . .

and jump . . .

and jump, until . . .

. . . big dogs come!

The puddle is all sploshed away.

And Ruffles is wet and cold and cross.

But Ruby shakes . . . and wags her tail. She still wants to play!

Ruffles doesn't. No. No.

No. No. No.

Now Ruby is sad.

So she goes away.

And Ruffles is **all alone.**

But here's Ruby again!
With Ruffles' new coat!

Ruffles will do **anything** for Ruby, even if . . .

it takes . . .   a really long time . . .   and he has to do . . .

lots and . . .   lots of . . .   wriggling.

Until . . .   at last!   The coat is on . . .

. . . and **look!**

Another puddle!

Maybe the new coat is not so bad after all.

Ruffles loves . . .

sniffing . . .

patting . . .

licking . . .

splishing . . .

splashing . . .

sploshing . . .

and jumping . . .

in puddles . . .

but, most of all . . .

Ruffles **loves** . . .

Ruby!